*Blessed are those who hunger and thirst
for righteousness, for they will be filled.*

—Matthew 5:6

The Berenstain Bears Go to Sunday School
Copyright © 2008 by Berenstain Bears, Inc.
Illustrations © 2008 by Berenstain Bears, Inc.

Requests for information should be addressed to:
Zonderkidz, Grand Rapids, Michigan 49530

Library of Congress Cataloging-in-Publication Data
Berenstain, Michael.
  The Berenstain Bears go to Sunday school / created by Stan and Jan Berenstain ; written by Mike
Berenstain.
     p. cm.
  Summary: Mama Bear decides it has been too long since they have attended church at the Chapel in
the Woods, so they all get up extra early and go.
  ISBN-13: 978-0-310-71248-0 (softcover)
  ISBN-10: 0-310-71248-3 (softcover)
  [1. Church attendance--Fiction. 2. Sunday schools--Fiction. 3. Bears--Fiction. 4. Christian life--Fiction.]
I. Berenstain, Stan, 1923- II. Berenstain, Jan, 1923- III. Title.
  PZ7.B44827Bg 2008
  [E]--dc22

                                                                                  2006033951

Zonderkidz is a trademark of Zondervan.

Editor: Bruce Nuffer
Art direction: Sarah Molegraaf

Printed in U.S.A.

08 09 10 11 • 9 8 7 6 5

The Berenstain Bears®
Go to Sunday School

Created by Stan and Jan Berenstain
Written by Mike Berenstain

ZONDER**kidz**

ZONDERVAN.com/
AUTHORTRACKER
follow your favorite authors

Sunday morning was a busy time in the big tree house down a sunny dirt road deep in Bear Country. The Bear family had things to do and places to go. Brother had soccer practice at ten thirty, and Sister had a ballet lesson at eleven. Usually Mama dropped them off before taking Honey Bear along to do some grocery shopping. Papa stayed home to get his fix-up chores done early so he could watch football in the afternoon.

But it hadn't always been that way for the Bear family. A few years back, before they'd gotten involved with so many activities, the Bear family had gone every Sunday morning to services at the Chapel in the Woods. Of course, that meant Brother and Sister went to Sunday school.

Mama Bear missed those days. It seemed to her that the family was a lot closer back then. Going to the Chapel in the Woods was like a kind of glue that held the whole family together.

Mama decided it was time for a little family conference. They all gathered in the living room one Saturday night, and she told them what was on her mind.

"Glue?" said Sister, puzzled. "You mean like when you glued that lamp back together after we broke it?"

"That's a very good example," said Papa. "That lamp gave us light. We glued it back together so we wouldn't be left in the dark. Worshiping God gives us light and warmth too. And our family needs a little glue from time to time to keep it together."

Sister and Brother thought that one over. It made sense ... sort of.

"Besides," said Mama, "I believe that going to church together is more important than all our other Sunday morning activities combined."

"More important than soccer?" gasped Brother, shocked.

"Or ballet?" chimed in Sister.

"Yes," Mama nodded firmly. "But don't get too excited. We'll go to the early service at eight thirty. That way, you'll have plenty of time to get to your soccer and ballet."

"Eight thirty in the morning?" cried Brother and Sister, even more upset. "That means we'll have to get up at seven o'clock—on the weekend!"

"Now, now," said Papa. He prided himself on always getting up early. "Early to bed and first to get up, makes a bear healthy, wealthy and ... uh ... how does that go?"

"Sleepy!" said Brother.

At breakfast the next morning, the Bear family did seem sleepy indeed. At least Brother and Sister did. They could hardly keep their eyes open. Papa wasn't exactly all there either. He was almost invisible behind his Sunday paper.

"Coffee, dear?" asked Mama, lifting the coffee pot.

"Uh!" grunted Papa, holding his cup out without looking up.

"Ahem!" said Mama.

"Huh—wha?" asked Papa, looking up. "Oh, sorry, my dear!" he said, folding the paper. "I guess I'm not really awake until I've had my morning coffee."

Mama got her purse and put on her best Sunday hat. They climbed down the front steps, and Papa put Honey Bear in her stroller. The whole family headed down the road to the Chapel in the Woods.

Other families joined them as they walked along. There were their neighbors Farmer and Mrs. Ben. They saw Uncle Willie, Aunt Min, and Cousin Fred from down the street.

They even ran into Too-Tall Grizzly being hauled along by his parents, Two-Ton and Too-Too Grizzly.

The Chapel in the Woods was nestled in a pretty little glen down by the creek. On this fresh spring morning, the dogwoods were in bloom. Papa began to hum a tune. Then he started to sing, "Come to the church by the wildwood. Oh, come to the church in the vale."

Mama joined in, "No spot is so dear to my childhood ..."

They finished together, "As the little brown church in the vale."

"What weird song is that?" asked Sister.

"Oh, it's just something we used to sing in church, together, when we were children," sighed Mama. "That was a long time ago."

"Did you know each other way back then?" asked Brother.

"Know each other!" laughed Papa. "Why, I was sweet on your mother when we were only eight years old. She was the cutest cub in the whole Sunday school. Once, I brought a frog into class. I was going to let it loose during the story of the plagues of Egypt. But I decided it would be funnier to slip it down Mama's back—it was too!"

Brother's and Sister's eyes widened, imagining the scene. "Wow!" they breathed softly.

"Now, dear," said Mama. "Let's not give the children any bright ideas."

They dropped Honey Bear off at the church nursery and filed quietly into the chapel. There was soft music playing on the organ as they found a pew. Then Preacher Brown climbed into the pulpit, and the service began.

"Welcome, friends!" said the preacher. "Let us join together in worship! Let us give thanks for this day the Lord has made!"

They all rose to sing a hymn. "Come to the church by the wildwood," sang the whole congregation. "Oh, come to the church in the vale."

"How about that?" whispered Brother to Sister. "They're still singing that same old song."

After the hymn and a prayer, and a little more organ music and some bell ringing, it was time for Sunday school.

Brother and Sister joined the other cubs as they trooped out of the chapel under the watchful eye of Preacher Brown.

Old Missus Ursula Bruinsky was the Sunday school teacher. Brother and Sister wondered just how old she was. She looked old enough to have been Mama and Papa's Sunday school teacher.

"Good morning, children," she said with a big smile. "Today we're going to learn the story of Noah's Ark." She looked around at them brightly. "Do any of you young'uns know the story of Noah's Ark?"

Cousin Fred, who read the dictionary for fun, raised his hand.

"Excellent, Fred!" said Missus Ursula. "Why don't you tell us the story?"

So Cousin Fred told the story of Noah's Ark. "Long, long ago, God saw that the people of the earth had become wicked. But Noah was a just man, and he walked with God. So God told Noah to build a great boat—an ark. God was going to bring a terrible flood upon all the earth.

And God told Noah to bring two of every sort of creature, male and female, into the ark. So Noah built the ark, gathered the animals, and went into it with his family."

Brother Bear interrupted. "Do you think they brought frogs into the ark?" he asked.

Missus Ursula laughed. "Why, I'm sure that Noah brought frogs into the ark, Brother Bear," she said, her eyes twinkling. "But if you think that you are going to bring a frog into this classroom the way your father did, young man, you have got another thing coming!"

Brother's mouth dropped wide open. Missus Ursula really was old enough to have been Mama and Papa's Sunday school teacher!

Cousin Fred went on with the story. "Then it began to rain. It rained for forty days and forty nights. All the earth was covered with the flood. And all living things, except those on the ark, died. After many months, Noah sent forth a dove. The dove came back carrying an olive leaf. Noah knew that the flood had passed. He let all of the animals go. Then God set a rainbow in the sky and promised Noah that he would never cover all the earth with the waters of a flood again."

The cubs all sighed. They were thinking back to the last big thunderstorm they'd had when the river went up over its banks and washed out the bridge. There had been a beautiful rainbow after that storm too.

"All right, cubs," said Missus Ursula. "Let's see if you can all draw pictures of the story of Noah's Ark."

There were crayons and paper on the tables, so the cubs set busily to work. Sister drew a beautiful picture of the ark resting on the mountaintop.

Brother drew a dramatic scene of rain pouring down with bolts of lightning and the ark tossing on the waves.

Too-Tall drew a picture of all the animals sticking their heads out of the ark, yelling "PEW!"

"Now, Too-Tall," said Missus Ursula. "I really don't think that's very appropriate." But Sister noticed her smiling, just the same, when she thought none of the cubs were looking.

Then, Sunday school was over. "Goodbye, cubs!" called Missus Ursula. "See you all next Sunday!"

The cubs ran outside, shouting and jumping after sitting still for so long. The grown-ups were coming out of the chapel. Preacher Brown was shaking hands with everyone, and folks were laughing and talking together.

And everyone joined in, "No spot is so dear to my childhood as the little brown church in the vale!"

"YAY!" shouted Honey Bear, wanting to join in too. And they all gave her a nice round of applause.

"There!" said Mama as they headed for home. "That wasn't too bad, was it?"

"No," said Sister. "In fact, it was kind of interesting."

"Yeah," agreed Brother, running on ahead. "And now … soccer!"

"And ballet!" added Sister.

"And football!" said Papa.

Mama rolled her eyes.

Sister began to hum, then sing softly, "Come to the church by the wildwood. Oh, come to the church in the vale."

Papa began to sing along, in rhythm, "Oh, come, come, come, come …"